your ball, Spot. We're at the circus now.

It's okay.
I've got it!

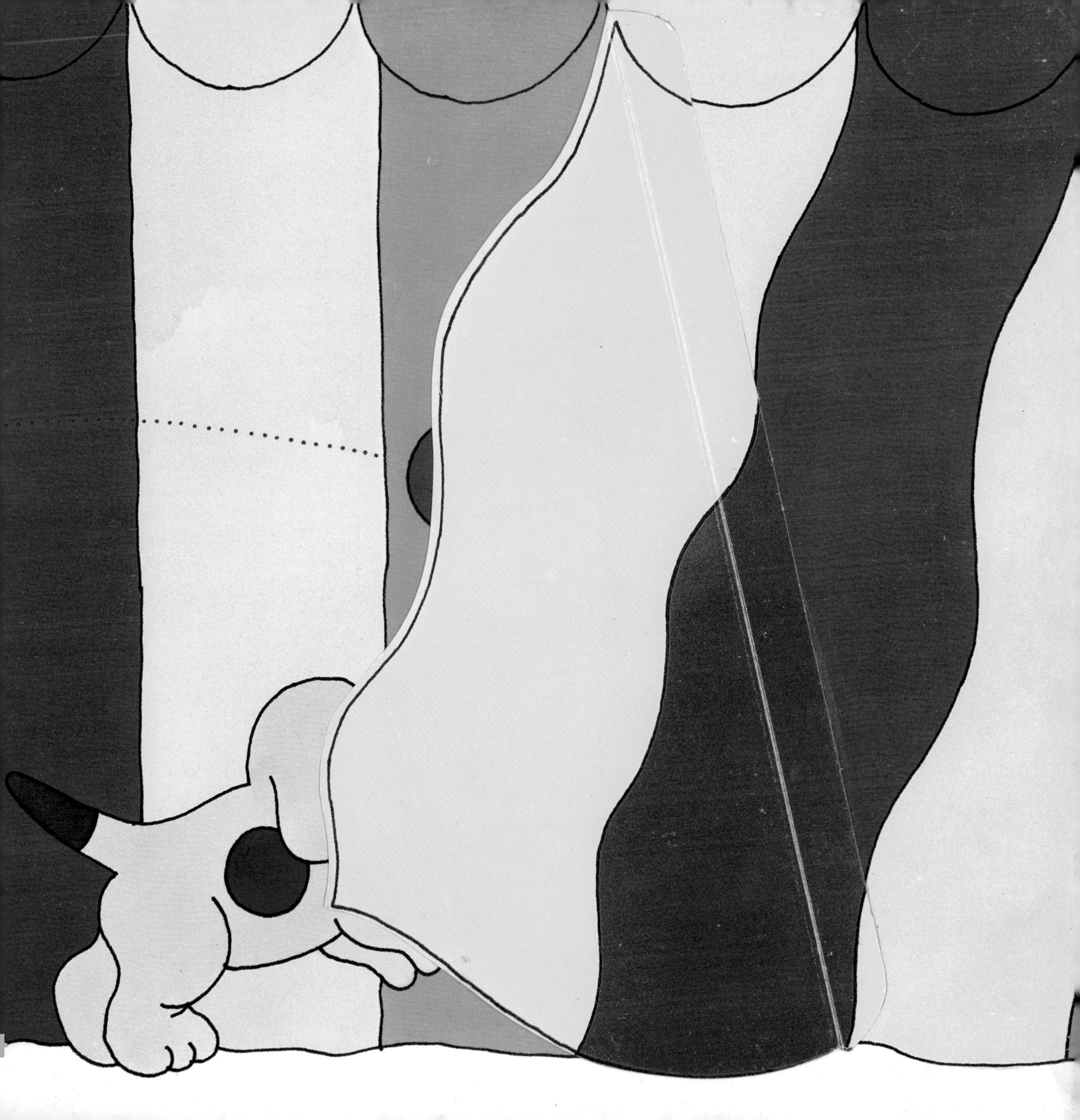

Excuse me, did you see my ball go by?

There it goes!
I wonder who
lives in here.

KEEP OUT

Please, do you have my ball?

I hope you didn't swallow my ball...

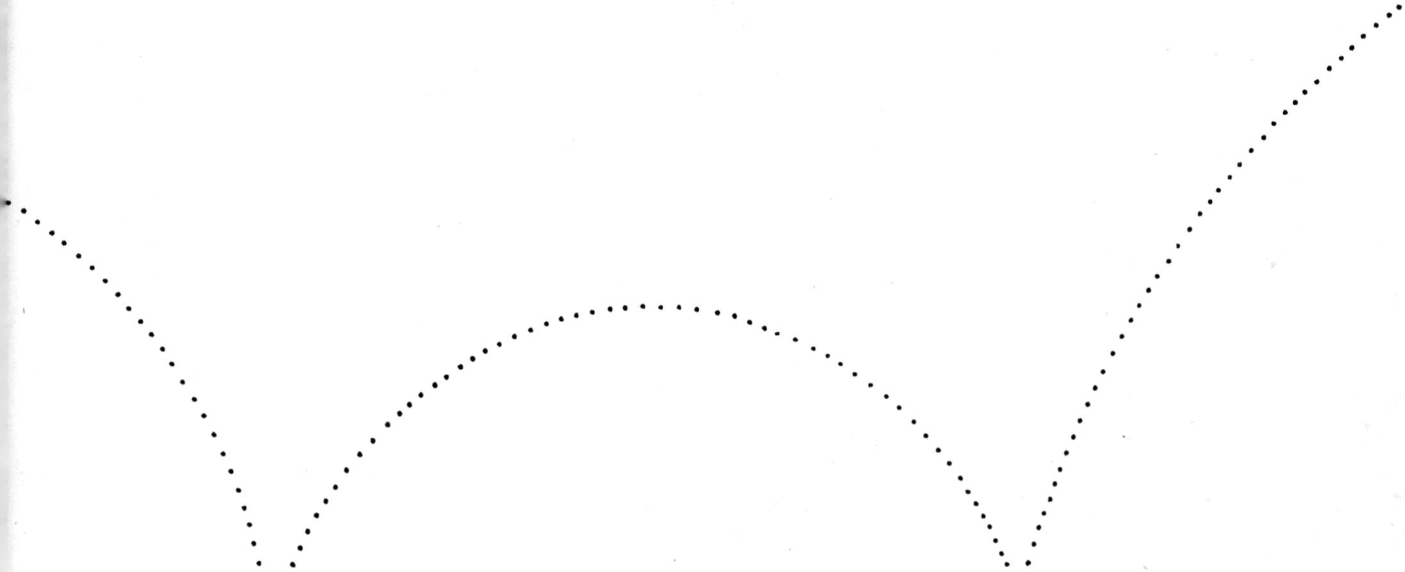

There it is!

Have you seen my ball?

Hurray!
Catch it!

At last! Spot has found his ball.

Spot